# A Simple Business Dinner

## *Other plays by the same author in English*

An innocent little murder

Casket for two

Cheaters

Crisis and Punishment

Critical but stable

Friday the 13th

Him and Her

Lovestruck at Swindlemore Hall

Quarantine

Running on Empty

Strip Poker

The Worst Village in England

JEAN-PIERRE MARTINEZ

# A Simple Business Dinner

English translation by

*Anne-Christine Gasc*

La Comédiathèque
*comediatheque.net*

## *Characters*

The CEO
The Hostess
The Minister

***You must obtain the authorisations from the author prior to any public performance, whether by professional or amateur companies : https://comediatheque.net***


ISBN 978-2-37705-808-2

*A bourgeois living room. Flowers on a small table. A painting on a wall. A table set for three. A mobile someone has forgotten somewhere, rings. A man enters wearing only boxer shorts and a dress shirt, fixing his tie. He picks up the mobile and takes the call.*

**CEO** – Yes James ... No, his Private Secretary just called, he's still in Parliament and won't be here for another half hour. Which is just as well because my suit is still at the cleaners. I hope it's not a sign ... If I can't get him to sign this bloody contract tonight that's where I'll end up, old boy: at the cleaners! And I'll take you down with me. We're in the middle of a financial crisis! And we're this close from putting the key under the door! Did you manage to sort out the girl? ...She should already be here, where the fuck is she? I need time to brief her before the Minister gets here ... By the way, your idea of bringing in an escort? Pure genius. I have to admit I wasn't keen on the idea at first, but after I met your ... Annabelle, is it? ... it completely changed my mind. The mental image of her holding his pen is ... His pen! To sign the contract! Absolutely, very high class. It's very important the Minister doesn't find out she's a professional. Because on top of everything else, this letch is convinced he's a stud! (*A doorbell rings*) Excuse me for a second, I have to get the door. I think that's her ...

*The CEO, still in boxer shorts, opens the door.*

**Hostess** – Mister Adam Sugar?

**CEO** – Yes ...

**Hostess** – Emmanuelle ... From the agency.

**CEO** – Emmanuelle? But ... I was expecting Annabelle. And you don't look like her at all ... Annabelle was a lot more ... I mean, a lot less ...

**Hostess** – Annabelle asked me to present her excuses. She was ... held up. I am filling in for her.

**CEO** – Filling in for her?

**Hostess** – I am just as experienced, I assure you ...

**CEO** – Well, yes, but ... That's not at all what was planned ... And I said I wanted class, not ... classroom ...

**Hostess** – Well, I mean…

**CEO** – Never mind, come on in ... don't just stand there, we'll sort it out ...

*The hostess enters. Young and pretty, but dressed in a very formal school uniform (duffle coat, white blouse, tartan skirt falling below the knees, high socks and polished mary-janes).*

**Hostess** – Thank you ...

**CEO** (*picking up his mobile again)* – James? Fuck… we're off to a bad start: the agency didn't send the girl I asked for ... How could you fuck this up? You should see what this one looks like ... (*Martin looks at the hostess up and down, appalled)* Well, how can I put this ...? (*To the hostess)* Please excuse me for a minute… (*He moves towards the room he came out of when he opened the door)* Listen, it's a shit show ... (*More quietly)* Even taking into account his sexual appetite and very pervy mind, I really don't think the promise of spending the night with this dope is going to be an incentive to sign a three billion pound contract ... She looks like she just walked straight out of a nun's boarding school ...

*He leaves. The hostess remains alone, a little unsettled and looks around the living room. Her mobile rings and she picks up.*

**Hostess** – Isabelle? Yes, yes, I just got there. But I barely had time to talk to him, actually ... Listen, I don't really understand ... When he saw me he seemed gutted… Like if he ordered a margherita pizza with extra hot sauce and they delivered a gluten-free vegetarian ... I'm the pizza in this analogy ... Are you sure you can't make it? Oh, right ... So basically you double-booked yourself for this evening… Yes, it happens ... No, of course you can't cut and paste yourself ... Hey, this is a pretty classy place, huh? Who's this guy again…? Adam Sugar? The construction company guy, you mean…? Oh, wow ... And you really think that I ... No, no, don't worry, I'm here, I might as well stay ... But you owe me a favour ... No, I'm not forgetting the three months of rent I owe you ... Speaking of which, he insists on calling you Annabelle ... Oh ...? I didn't know you needed a stage name to serve appetizers ... I don't need to tell you I have zero experience working as a French maid … Sure, a hostess, whatever ... Actually, when I told him I had a lot of experience he didn't seem to believe me. I think he could tell right away I'd never done this before in my life ... He commented on my outfit too ... I don't understand ... You told me to dress like I normally do ... Something classic and smart ... That's what I did ... I thought they were going to provide the waitress uniform, like they do at the Agricultural Fair ... Hang on, he's coming back ...

*The CEO returns, this time he's fully dressed.*

**CEO** – Well ... Never mind, it'll have to do because we're running out of time. (*He scrutinises the hostess again)* And at the end of the day, this Little Miss Goody Two Shoes look might just work. It's very realistic, well done! You absolutely can't tell that you're really a ... Well, you know what I mean ... Right, so let me explain the situation, real quick. I am Adam Sugar, CEO of Stonewall Construction.

**Hostess** – Oh, wow! That's only the largest construction company in the UK. (*Quoting the company's slogan)* Don't be stonewalled, invest in Stonewall!

**CEO** – Very good ... I see the agency also requires a certain level of culture ... That way we can save time and skip over the basics ... So, tonight I am having a politician over for dinner and we want him to sign a very large contract ... This contract right here (*He shows her the contract)*. I'm talking about the Minister of Transportation ...

**Hostess** (*surprised)* – John Fiddle-Koch?

*She mispronounces the last name as* Cock.

**CEO** (*correcting her pronunciation*) – It's pronounced *Coke*. Also known as JFK.

**Hostess** – Because the press believes he's the favourite to become our next Prime Minister ...

**CEO** – That's pretty much all they have in common ... because he sure doesn't look like John Fitzgerald Kennedy, if you know what I mean. But thankfully for us, like Kennedy, JFK loves women. So you can just pretend you're Marilyn Monroe … Even if you're no Marilyn yourself either, huh?

**Hostess** – No ...

**CEO** – For privacy reasons, I organised this little get-together at my residence. It's rather inconvenient for me as you can imagine. But fancy hotels aren't known for their discretion, you know what it's like …

**Hostess** – Yes ... Actually, no ...

**CEO** – Nowadays, if the tabloids print a photo of a Minister stepping out of the Four Seasons or the Savoy, it's worse than if he was seen coming out of a place that rents rooms by the hour.

**Hostess** – Ah, yes ...

**CEO** – So while my wife is visiting her mother for a few days in Brighton, I have an opportunity ...

**Hostess** – Mmm…

**CEO** – I'd just as rather she didn't know anything about this ... She's very jealous ...

**Hostess** – Of course ...

**CEO** – So anyway ... You're here to ... ensure the Minister is in the best possible mindset to sign this contract with our company rather than our main competitor ... Is that clear?

**Hostess** – Er, yes ...

*The CEO, a little embarrassed, takes out a wad of notes from his pocket and hands it to her.*

**CEO** – Here you go ... This is what we agreed with Annabelle ... Half now and the rest ... upon completion.

**Hostess** (*taking the money)* – Completion?

*The CEO's mobile rings again.*

**CEO** – Yes ? Yes, Minister ... (*He motions to the hostess to excuse him for a moment and leaves the room again)* Yes, yes, of course ... No problem at all ... Very well, Minister ... But of course, Minister ...

*Alone once again, the hostess grabs her mobile and presses a key.*

**Hostess** (*delighted)* – Isabelle? But this job is amazing! He just gave me a wad of notes this thick, I didn't even have time to count them. And he said he'd give me the same again later ... After the food has been delivered ... Wow… Never realised catering paid this well ... I'll be able to pay you back the three months rent I owe you and still have enough to pay back some of my student loan! You know, seeing all this cash made me think, like ... What was the point of killing myself studying for the entrance exam to the London Business School? I should have gone to culinary school ... (*She looks around her again and sees the table dressed for three)* I'm not even sure what he expects from me anymore ... I thought I was going to pour Champagne at a reception, but it looks more like they're having a threesome ... No idea who the third one is ... What do you mean, not just pouring the Champagne? What else?

*The conversation is interrupted by the CEO who returns, and she puts her mobile away.*

**CEO** – The Minister will be downstairs in a minute with his chauffeur and his bodyguards. I'm going down to meet him on the steps. Sorry, I really don't have time to tell you more. But you're the expert, you can make it up as you go along. Your colleague told me the agency also gave you improv classes ... (*He's about to leave)* Do I need to remind you that this needs to remain very classy? Use charm, but never vulgar. Oh, one last thing ... Your name will be ... Mirabelle. I'm sorry, but you really don't look like an Emmanuelle ...

**Hostess** – And you think I look like a Mirabelle…?

**CEO** – Emmanuelle, it's just a little too ... I mean, it's obvious it's not your real name.

*Disconcerted, the hostess looks towards the table.*

**Hostess** – Who's the third guest?

**CEO** – The third guest? But that's you! Did you think you were going to eat out of a bucket on the floor ...? I told you, everything has to be extremely high class…

**Hostess** – But ... So ... What do you want me to do, exactly?

**CEO** – All right, so during dinner you stick to general topics. You act like the daughter from a good family, a little dim but with an excellent upbringing. Then after dinner ... you pretend to fall for the git's charms!

**Hostess** – The git?

**CEO** – Listen, the less you know the more natural it'll look ... And I'll tell you what to do along the way, depending on whether the pig takes the bait or not ... Now I really have to go. I wouldn't want the Minister to wait ... We are here to cater to his every desire, Mirabelle ....

*The CEO leaves the room. She grabs her mobile immediately.*

**Hostess** – Isabelle? What did you get me into? That's not at all what we talked about! Now I have to have dinner with them and be some sort of Mata Hari! What the hell is this? Role play? An orgy? What do you mean, trust my instincts and everything will be fine? Yeah, well my instincts are screaming at me to run out the door! Listen, it's not my problem if you lose a big client! I had no idea what you did for a living, did I? I thought this was about serving clients, not servicing them!

*The CEO returns with the minister, who is wearing his MBE medal. The hostess is forced to put her mobile away.*

**CEO** – Come in, come in, please, Minister ... Make yourself at home ...

**Minister** – Thank you ... Excuse my tardiness but I was on a call with the Prime Minister ... About this little project of ours, actually ...

*The CEO enters the room with the minister, who notices the hostess.*

**Hostess** (*troubled)* – Mister Fiddle-Cock ...

**Minister** – It's pronounced Coke ... But you can call me John ...

**CEO** – Ah! It's my turn to apologise, Minister. My ... niece is in London for a few days… She'll be dining with us, if you don't mind that is ... Look at her ... I couldn't kick her out of bed ... I mean kick her out of the house ... I trust it won't be too much of a bother?

**Minister** (*leering)* – But not at all, not at all ...

**CEO** – And she was so excited at the thought of meeting you ... Weren't you, Mirabelle?

**Hostess** – Er ... Yes, Uncle ...

**Minister** – What a charming young thing ... And what does this young lady do?

*The CEO signals to the hostess that she should answer.*

**Hostess** – I ... I'm a student. At the London School of Business.

*The CEO discretely signals that this is a great idea.*

**Minister** – Very well, very well ... So maybe a future minister, huh…? But I thought you said she was just spending a few days in London?

**CEO** – Yes ...

**Minister** – But if she's studying at the London School of Economics ...

**CEO** (*improvising)* – The London School of Economics ... in Cardiff.

**Minister** – Oh really ...

**Hostess** – My mother is Welsh.

**CEO** – That would be my sister.

**Hostess** – I wanted to study in London, but ...

**CEO** – She didn't get in.

*Mirabelle cringes a little, offended.*

**Minister** – What a shame ... Well, I went to Oxford and look where that got me, Mirabelle ...

**Hostess** – Well, they say you're likely to be our next Prime Minister ...

**Minister** – They say so many things, you know … Anyway, tonight I have to spend the evening bartering with your uncle, this mean old scrooge, to find out how much he's going to charge me for every mile of this new motorway.

**CEO** – Come, come ... There's always room for discussion, you know that ... And we're almost amongst family, after all ...

**Minister** – What did I tell you ... I'm sure he's got a plan to get me drunk so I'll sign whatever offer he places in front of me ... But I won't be corrupted so easily …

**CEO** – Your reputation precedes you, Minister ... Your integrity is legendary ... And everyone knows of the great legacy you're leaving behind thanks to your resourcefulness ... I've even heard that in the corridors of Parliament they call you "the beaver lover" ...

**Minister** – Oh, really ... I didn't know that ... And I didn't know the beaver was the symbol of resourcefulness ...

**Hostess** – That's not why they call you that ...

**CEO** – But of course! The beaver is a great builder! And very resourceful! He fells trees with his teeth and builds dams with his tail…

**Minister** – Anyway, as you know, our country is facing a very difficult situation at the moment. If the United Kingdom needs my help, I won't shirk my responsibilities ...

**Hostess** – All to your credit, Minister.

**Minister** – I am sure, Miss, that, should the situation arise, you wouldn't hesitate to sacrifice yourself for Queen and country either, would you…?

**CEO** – Minister, please, have a seat. Mirabelle will get you something to drink. Won't you, darling?

**Hostess** – Some Champagne, maybe?

**Minister** – If it's to celebrate the signing of our contract, let me point out it's a little premature. You know the state of our country's finances ...

**CEO** – A little refreshment never hurt anyone! (*He signals to the hostess to fill the glasses)* And let me remind you that our company has already agreed to make significant cuts to our profit margin to reduce the cost of this project so as to spare the nation's deficit.

**Minister** – My good man, three billion pounds, that's still a tidy sum…

**CEO** – For one hundred miles of motorway! It's a steal, Minister, believe me! Look, if you can get it cheaper somewhere else within 28 days we'll refund the difference.

**Hostess** – Never knowingly undersold ...

**Minister** – As you well know, Miss, international credit rating agencies recently withdrew our country's AAA rating. These days, our Treasury Bonds are worth less than black pudding at your local butcher's. And international financial backers think the Prime Minister of this great nation is a coiled Cumberland sausage.

**CEO** – But my dear Minister, we firmly count on you to become the Cumberland sausage after the next General Election.

**Minister** – Flattering my ambition won't get you anywhere, my dear man ... I should even say my very dear man ... My too dear man!

**CEO** – Minister, that's just stonewalling.

**Hostess** – Don't be stonewalled, invest in Stonewall!

**CEO** – The UK's motorway network is our country's nervous system. Its blood circulation system! It brings British companies, the weary muscles of our great country, their daily supply of oxygen. As Minister of Transport you know that better than I do!

**Minister** – There's only the small matter of convincing the public and the media that a motorway linking Ealing to Ashbocking in Suffolk is a strategic priority for the recovery of our nation ...

**CEO** – What else are public relation teams for?

**Minister** – And we might not have hit rock bottom yet ... Excuse my French, Miss, but credit agencies have us by the short and curlies.

**CEO** – Come now ... The public coffers aren't empty yet. It's a very fair and mutually-beneficial contract, I assure you. Another glass of Champagne, Minister?

*He signals to the hostess to top up the minister's glass.*

**Minister** – Do you have any idea how much the annual interest would be if we were to borrow another three billion pounds? That's if the Chinese even agree to lend it to us ...

**CEO** – That's what motorway tolls are for! You'll be making money hand over fist! It's an endless source of revenue for you! I mean, for the country ...

**Minister** – Hmm ... What do you think, my dear child? (*Amused)* Let's see ... What would you do if you were Transport Minister instead of me?

**Hostess** – I always thought the state didn't think it through when they privatised the motorways ... Why sell off the goose that lays the golden eggs, all for a few ingots?

**Minister** – You might have a point there ...

**CEO** – Always listen to the youth!

**Minister** – The goose that lays the golden eggs ... (*Leering at the hostess)* Indeed, that's exactly the type of bird that every man dreams of having running around at his disposal ...

**CEO** – Well, tonight, Minister, it is my pleasure to offer you that bird on a platter…

**Minister** – Really ...?

**CEO** – Currently, the toll fees to drive from Manchester to London cost almost as much as a train ticket!

**Minister** – Are you sure ...?

**CEO** – And then there's the petrol and the driver ...

**Hostess** – Hmm ... Did you ever think that might actually be the problem ...?

**CEO** – Pardon?

**Hostess** – At this price, why would anyone want to take the motorway?

**Minister** – Especially to go from Ealing to Little Thurlow…

**Hostess** – Little Thurlow?

**CEO** – And yet ... We know how important this project is to you, Minister, don't we?

**Minister** – I won't disagree ...

**CEO** – You've been its most fierce supporter since the last General Elections ... And we all know why, of course ...

**Hostess** – We do ... ? Why ?

**CEO** – Well ... Two reasons. First, to allow easy access to Suffolk – which is, as we all know, one of the economic lungs of the UK.

**Hostess** – And the second reason ...?

**Minister** – Secondly because I am the MP for the Ashbocking constituency but I live in Ealing.

**CEO** – It will make for a much more pleasant commute between Parliament and your constituency.

**Hostess** (*ironically)* – Or even between Downing Street and your weekend residence…

*The CEO glares at her. Thankfully, the doorbell rings and creates a welcome disruption.*

**CEO** – That must be the catering company ... (*To the hostess)* Could you get the door, Mirabelle ...

**Hostess** – Of course, Uncle.

**Minister** – She's so sweet ... Yet she has some bite too ... Am I wrong?

**CEO** – Just like her mother ... but younger.

**Minister** – Er, yes ...

**CEO** – The privilege of youth ...

**Minister** – But very well brought up.

**CEO** – And housebroken ...

*The hostess returns carrying a large platter loaded with several plates that she places on the table.*

**Hostess** – Voila! Dinner is served ...

**CEO** – I ordered an assortment of cold cuts. I thought it would be easier. No need for staff to help with the service so we avoid any unwanted witnesses. I mean, unwanted eyes and ears ... Even when you have complete trust in your staff ...

**Minister** – Naturally ... I understand ... But this dinner isn't a secret, nor has anything reprehensible happened yet, has it? Unless you're planning to try to sweeten the deal with a bribe or two?

*The CEO clearly wonders whether the minister is joking or making a suggestion.*

**CEO** – Well ...

**Minister** – I'm joking, of course.

**CEO** – Of course.

**Minister** – The food looks delicious.

**CEO** – From the best deli in London! They are scandalously expensive, but ever so tasty ...

**Minister** – I can't resist, I'm ravenous. Even if this is getting dangerously close to the textbook definition of passive corruption.

*They all sit at the table.*

**Hostess** – Would you like a napkin if we're going to grease your hand? (*The minister is a little disconcerted and the CEO throws her a dirty look)*. I mean, if you get grease on your hands?

**Minister** – How can I refuse when it's offered so sweetly ... (*To the CEO)* She's charming ... So, Mirabelle, you live in Wales, is that right?

**Hostess** – I do ...? I mean, I do!

**CEO** – She lives in Cardiff ...

**Minister** – I can't hear a hint of an accent ...

**Hostess** – Well ... It's ... I took elocution lessons to try and lose it. You know what it's like, when you have a Welsh accent and you're hoping for a career in politics or in business ... even if it's more or less the same thing, nowadays ... It's immediately assumed you're a sheep-…

**Minister** – A sheep…?

**Hostess** – A sheep-shagger ...

*The CEO is smoldering.*

**Minister** – Indeed, there are a few black sheep everywhere, so to speak, yokels who don't know any better and damage the reputation of this stunning region. But a handful of people don't represent an entire country. I was a member of the Welsh Chamber of Commerce for about ten years. I know Cardiff very well…

**CEO** – Really ...?

**Minister** – What does your sister do in Cardiff?

**CEO** – My sister ...?

**Minister** – I know everyone there, you know.

**CEO** – What does she do ...? Er, yes ... (*Turning towards the hostess)* What is she doing these days?

**Hostess** – She's dead.

**CEO** – So she is ... I get so emotional when I talk about her ... I couldn't even say the word ...

**Minister** – I'm very sorry for your loss.

**CEO** – She was my sister, after all ... And I only had the one. I still have a few brothers, but ...

**Minister** – It's not the same thing ...

**CEO** – They can't replace her ...

**Hostess** – I also only had just one mother ...

**Minister** – Ah yes, that's ... Often the case, unfortunately ... And now she's dead ...

**CEO** – As a doornail ... An ... An accident ...

**Minister** – An accident?

**CEO** – A refrigerated lorry ... Crossing the street ... To get to the butcher's.

**Minister** – Oh my God ...

**CEO** – Yeah well, that's in the past, let's move on. It's what she would have wanted, and all that… Life goes on ... and so does construction work! You know what they say: it's not the end of the road!

**Minister** – And so this lovely young lady still lives in Cardiff?

**CEO** – That's right ... With her Mum ... Who's dead.

**Minister** – That reminds me ... There's an excellent restaurant in Cardiff where they serve the best Laverbread you've ever tasted ... What is it called again?

*Thankfully, the minister's mobile phone rings sparing the hostess from answering the question. The minister takes the call.*

**Minister** – Yes? Yes, yes ... No, no, you're not interrupting anything ... Hang on a minute ... (*To the CEO)* Please excuse me. Is there a place where I can take this call in private?

**CEO** – Yes, of course. This way, please ...

*The CEO shows him the way.*

**Minister** (*to the person he is speaking to)* – Yes, yes, I'm listening ...

*The minister leaves the room.*

**CEO** – Ok, so far so good ... I think you've managed to awaken this old perv's libido with your boarding school look straight out of a Madeline book… Just tone down the rebel side a little ...

**Hostess** – Don't worry, I won't do anything to jeopardize this negotiation ...

**CEO** – And now it's time to take your game to the next level, all right? Discrete and elegant only takes you so far, efficient and forward seals the deal.

**Hostess** – Forward?

**CEO** – So, you continue to bait the big fish ... and bam! You hook him when he least expects it. What you do, is you have to take him by surprise, you see. After that this old shark will be putty in your hands ... He loves fresh meat, believe me. On that front my intel is 100% reliable.

*His mobile phone rings and he picks up.*

**CEO** – Yes, James ... No, this really isn't a good time to talk ... I think the old letch isn't insensitive to the charms of schoolgirls in uniform ... By the way, did you know he spent ten years in Cardiff? You could have mentioned it! Would have avoided looking like an ass ... (*The minister returns).* Right, I've got to go ...

**Minister** – Please excuse me but I thought it best if you didn't overhear my conversation ... Do you know who that was?

**CEO** – No idea ...

**Minister** – Your biggest competitor ...

**CEO** – Well, what do you know ...

**Minister** – And to be honest, he made me an interesting offer ... a very interesting offer, actually.

**CEO** – How much?

**Minister** – Same as you ... but with twenty extra miles of motorway ...

**Hostess** – Ah yes, on a hundred miles long motorway that's twenty per cent more, that's a very interesting promotion, indeed.

**CEO** – Twenty more miles? But there's only hundred miles between Ealing and Little Thurlow! The surveyors' reports are all in agreement!

**Minister** – Your competitor is offering a slightly different route, one that passes through West Mercy. That's where my mother lives ... (*To the hostess)* And you of all people should know how important it is to be able to visit your Mum every once in a while, while she's still alive… (*The minister's mobile phone rings again and he takes the call).* Yes ... (*To the CEO)* Excuse me again ... Yes, yes, I'm listening ...

*He goes into the next room.*

**CEO** – We're fucked ...

**Hostess** – Just give him his twenty percent extra, like they do with corn flakes ...

**CEO** – That's impossible ... Our costs are already the lowest they can be ... Adding twenty more miles for the same price will eat all our profits.

**Hostess** – But you'll be restarting the economy! Think of the country's economic growth!

**CEO** – But out shareholders don't give a shit about growth! What they expect at the end of the fiscal year is big, fat dividends! Hang on ... Why am I even discussing this with a whore who's just here as a promotional incentive to help with the contract signature!

**Hostess** – A whore?

**CEO** – Just do your fucking job, okay? I paid for the services of an escort, not for a TED talk by Warren Buffet!

**Hostess** – An escort?

**CEO** – Everything relies on you from now on, do you understand? You must absolutely convince him that your undercarriage is more interesting than a dual carriageway connecting his house to his mother's care home!

**Hostess** – Listen here, Mister, I think there's been a misunderstanding ... I'm filling in for a friend who evidently hasn't been entirely candid about what would be expected of me during this work placement ... I am not a prostitute! I am really a student at the London School of Economics, and I take on side jobs to afford rent and tuition, that's all.

**CEO** – Is this a joke…?

**Hostess** – Let me rephrase it. I'll give you back your money and then I'll get the hell out of here ... Clear enough now?

**CEO** – Hang on, no need to get all worked up ... Please forgive me. Can you listen to me for a minute? Please?

**Hostess** – Oh, I'll listen to you but that won't change anything to the fact that I don't sleep with men for money ... Actually, I don't sleep around very much at all ... Even for free ...

**CEO** – If this contract isn't signed tonight, our shareholders will vote to close down the motorway department of this company in order to focus on other more profitable departments. Hundreds of employees will lose their jobs. Including me, to be perfectly honest with you ...

**Hostess** – I'm sorry, you must have me confused with someone who cares.

**CEO** – You're my last trump card, Mirabelle.

**Hostess** – Emmanuelle.

**CEO** – Everything relies on you. Workers will lose their livelihoods! Their entire families will be evicted, thrown out on the street! Their children won't have the same opportunities to study like you did!

**Hostess** – Enough, you're going to make me cry ... I'm not going to accept a hookup just to prevent a redundancy plan!

**CEO** – Who said anything about a hookup…? Our deal is only that you get this tosser to sign the contract. If you can do that without sleeping with him, too bad for him ... I mean, good for you ...

**Hostess** – And how would that work?

**CEO** – You start by offering him a drink, then you whet his appetite with the entrée and at the last moment you withhold dessert. Just as long as you get him to pay the bill before leaving…

**Hostess** – I don't know what to say ...

**CEO** – He seems to enjoy his drink. So if you can get him to hit the bottle ...

**Hostess** *(hurt)* – Are you suggesting he has to be three sheets to the wind to want to sleep with me? First you call me a whore, now this ... You really know how to talk to women ...

*The CEO's mobile phone rings. He takes the call.*

**CEO** – What the fuck, James! This girl you sent me doesn't want to put out! *(Immediately softening his voice)* Honey? Is that you? I wasn't expecting your call ... So, what's the weather like in Brighton? It's nighttime ... Yes, here too ... What was what? A girl? What girl? No, of course not ... But honey, you know that I would never ... Hello? Hello? She hung up… Just what I needed ... What a shitshow ... I need to call her back immediately ...

*The CEO leaves to call his wife. The hostess quickly calls someone on her mobile.*

**Hostess** – What is this trap you sent me in? I'm not a whore! ... A glamour hostess? I'm sorry, from where I'm standing, I can't really see the difference. If I'd known I never would have accepted! I bet that's why you chose to withhold significant details about this job ... Yes, you told me the agency was called Glamour International ... No, I'm sorry but I didn't connect the dots ... What about my three months rent? So, either I sleep with this fat pig or you kick me out, is that it?

*The minister returns, forcing her to end her conversation abruptly and to put her mobile phone away.*

**Minister** – Are you alone?

**Hostess** – My ... uncle had to make an urgent phone call ... A small misunderstanding with his wife ...

**Minister** – That'll give us a bit of time to chat and get to know each other. You'll have to give me your phone number. In case you get laid ...

**Hostess** – In case I get laid ...?

**Minister** – In case you get laid off, I mean... If you need another student job, or even full-time employment after you graduate, don't hesitate to contact me. I'll give you my personal number. Only a handful of people have it, you know.

**Hostess** – Thank you so much for this privilege ...

**Minister** – We have to help the youth. I don't know why but I have a feeling we're going to get along really well, don't you? You have spunk ... I like that ... And if my party wins the next General Elections, I'll need to surround myself with a new team. Younger ... Open to new experiences ... Willing to try anything ...

**Hostess** – And with sharp tongues ...

**Minister** – You're not going to believe this but our Chancellor can barely write ... And he can't add large numbers without the help of his Parliamentary Secretary and two or three accountants ... (*He takes her by the waist)* How would you like to join my campaign staff?

**Hostess** – They say you're the British JFK, but in reality you're more like Bill Clinton ...

*The minister moves closer to the hostess.*

**Minister** – I do like a bit of backtalking ...

*She smacks him across the face. The CEO returns.*

**CEO** – How's everything going ...?

*The minister pulls himself together.*

**Minister** – To be honest, I am a little embarrassed, my dear friend ...

**CEO** – I'm sure we'll be able to come to an arrangement ... Unfortunately, I can't give you the extra miles on that connecting access road to West Mercy. (*Looking at the hostess)* But there might be another way to sweeten the deal…

*The hostess glares at him, indicating how inappropriate his comment is.*

**Minister** – I just heard from my mother. That was her calling just now ...

**CEO** – Oh ... And your dear mother is doing well, I hope ...

**Minister** – Alas ... She's starting to lose her mind ... She thinks I'm already Prime Minster…

**Hostess** – But … Minister, that just means she's a visionary! It's the opposite of Alzheimer ... She isn't forgetting the past, she's remembering the future ...

**Minister** – Unfortunately, she also thinks I'm in jail for inappropriate relations with a minor ...

**Hostess** – Ah, yes ... That really makes no sense at all.

**CEO** – If you were Prime Minister, you'd have complete immunity from prosecution.

**Hostess** – That's not why you're running… is it?

**Minister** – Anyway, I'm afraid my poor mother will be relying on me even more in the coming years. We can't just abandon our elders, can we?

**CEO** – No, of course not ...

**Minister** – I make a point of visiting her at least once a week. Of course, with this new motorway taking me right to her, it'll be even easier ...

**Hostess** – Couldn't you find her a care home in Ealing?

**Minister** – Unfortunately, you know how old people are ... They like things to be just so ... I'm afraid that moving her now would create such an upheaval in her life that it would drag her in a downwards spiral ...

**CEO** – I can understand that ... What I don't understand, however, is how our main competitor can afford such a deal ...

**Hostess** – Maybe his crews are all working off the books ... Apparently, it's quite common in the construction industry ...

**Minister** – Er, I'd rather not know about this ...

**Hostess** – That's surprising, because the government actually sends agents to track down employers with cash-in-hand employment practices ...

**Minister** – She's adorable ... But you know how it is ... We all have our own ways to appease our conscience ... Don't tell me that your dear mother never hired a cleaner off the books…

**Hostess** – My dear mother is dead.

**Minister** – Oh, that's right, forgive me ... (*To the CEO)* But back to our contract, my friend. As I was telling you, I really want to make this work. We're so close! Twenty extra miles of motorway, what is that worth to you, really?

**CEO** – Six hundred million pounds ...

**Minister** – And the state will be eternally grateful, believe me. I, myself, am willing to show my appreciation ...

**CEO** – Really?

*The minister points to the MBE medal on his lapel.*

**Minister** – How would you like one of these?

*The CEO seems tempted for an instant.*

**CEO** – Of course it's tempting, but ...

**Minister** – I'm sure your wife would be very impressed ... not to mention your niece.

**CEO** – For sure ... (*Coming back to reality)* But six hundred million pounds for an MBE ... I don't think our shareholders would be as impressed as my wife ...

**Hostess** – Come now, you're under estimating yourself, Uncle!

**Minister** – And these extra twenty miles will do so much to help old age pensioners!

**Hostess** – Those living in Framlingham in particular ...

**CEO** – My shareholders are mostly American pension funds, I'm afraid ...

**Minister** – I'll let you think about it ... But quickly. Your competitor is willing to do anything to win this contract, you know ... In the meantime, I wouldn't say no to a little tart.

**CEO** – I was just going to suggest we bring in dessert ...

*The minister's mobile phone rings again and he takes the call.*

**Minister** – Yes…? Oh, yes ... But, of course, with pleasure ... No, not at all, quite the contrary ... We'll be among family ... Very well, I'll call you as soon as I'm on my way ...

*The minister puts his mobile away.*

**CEO** – Not more bad news from your mother, I hope?

**Minister** – No, nothing like that ... Thank you for your concern ... Actually, you should be concerned ... It was your competitor again ... Ivan. The CEO of the Woodwall construction company…

**CEO** – Oh ...

**Minister** – He's inviting me for cocktails at his home later this evening, to present his counter offer ... Funnily enough, he asked me if it was okay if his goddaughter joined us ... Everyone seems very keen to introduce their relatives all of a sudden ...

**Hostess** – It's half term ...

*The CEO, worried, signals to the hostess to get on with it.*

**Minister** – So? What kind of treats are you offering?

**CEO** – I believe we have a variety of tea pastries. You won't be disappointed ... Mirabelle?

**Hostess** – So, we have a raspberry fool and a spotted dick ... both very fitting ...

**CEO** – The French fancies, on the other hand, have your name all over them.

**Minister** – Excellent, excellent ... (*He stuffs a few pastries in his mouth)*. French fancies are my guilty pleasure ...

**CEO** – Please, take a seat. Make yourself comfortable ...

*They all sit around the table. The CEO signals again to the hostess that she should get on with the programme. But she clearly doesn't know what to say or do.*

**Hostess** – So, you wouldn't mind letting the state enter into a binding agreement with a company employing illegal workers? I would have thought that someone hoping to become our next Prime Minister ... I am very disappointed ... I was actually considering voting for your party ...

*The CEO rolls his eyes.*

**Minister** (*with his mouth full of food)* – My sweet summer child. You'll soon learn that in politics, compromises are the basis of every successful negotiation. Speaking of compromise, I'll take some more of this excellent Champagne ...

*The CEO motions to the hostess that she should top up the minister's glass, which she does.*

**CEO** – I have it shipped specially from France. I have a few cases in the cellar, if you'd like some ...

**Minister** – In any case, I won't decide anything until I've spoken with your competitor ...

**Hostess** – And his goddaughter ...

**CEO** – Would her name be Annabelle, by any chance ...?

**Minister** – Do you know her?

**CEO** – No, no, I mean… Please, there's still a few pastries left ...

**Minister** – With pleasure.

*The minister stuffs his face again. The CEO starts playing footsies with the minister who, thinking it's the hostess, is visibly excited.*

**Hostess** – You seem to be enjoying that.

**Minister** – I shouldn't, really ... but it's nice to stray from the straight and narrow once in a while ...

*To her surprise, he winks at her.*

**Minister** – Delicious, really delicious ... This sweet little tart ...

**CEO** – But Minister, I see your glass is empty again ... Mirabelle?

*Mirabelle stands to grab the bottle from the Champagne bucket. The CEO pulls his foot away a second too late. Slightly drunk, the minister wonders if it was really the hostess's foot. The hostess sits back down.*

**Hostess** – More Champagne?

*The minister's foot reaches for the hostess's as she's pouring his drink. Surprised, she more or less deliberately spills the champagne on his lap instead of his glass. The minister jumps out of his chair.*

**Hostess** – Oh, I'm sorry ... I'm so clumsy ...

**Minister** – Could you point me to the bathroom ...?

**CEO** – I am so very sorry ... This way, please ... At the end of the corridor, to the right ...

*The minister leaves. The CEO is outraged. He brings a mop from the next room and hands it to the hostess so she can mop the Champagne that's on the floor.*

**CEO** – Do you really think that pouring Champagne on his lap is the best way to encourage his ardours ...?

*The hostess takes the mop and wipes the floor.*

**Hostess** – I'm sorry, a reflex. He was playing footsie ...

**CEO** – But that's excellent! It means he's taking the bait. Don't tell me that you can't even handle a few close encounters under the table. Now you just need to hook him in.

**Hostess** (*the mop in her hand)* – Hook him in?

**CEO** – Listen, I think I know how to fix this and also speed things up a little ...

**Hostess** – Do I want to hear this ....?

**CEO** – In a minute I'll pretend to get a call on my mobile and I'll make up an excuse to leave the two of you together ...

**Hostess** – You're going to leave me alone with this rutting goat?

**CEO** – Rutting cabinet Minister ...

**Hostess** – I stand corrected.

*He waves the contract in her face.*

**CEO** – Listen, just get him to sign this contract. And before he jumps your bones, you make up and excuse and you leave ...

**Hostess** – What kind of excuse?

**CEO** – I don't know… Anything ... A text message saying your mother just had an accident, for example.

**Hostess** – Are you for real?

**CEO** – Why? What's wrong?

**Hostess** – My mother's already dead!

**CEO** – I'm so sorry for your loss, I had no idea ...

**Hostess** – That's what you told him earlier!

**CEO** – Oh, that's right ... Well, er ... Tell him I had an accident and that you have to go to see me in hospital!

**Hostess** – That's a lousy plan.

**CEO** – Do you have a better one?

**Hostess** – Do you have a maid?

**CEO** – I gave her the night off so we could be alone ... But anyway, she's in her fifties and looks like the bridge troll, with a triple chin and facial hair, so I don't think that ...

**Hostess** – Is she a live-in maid?

**CEO** – Yes, her room is one floor up, right above us, actually.

**Hostess** – All right, so you pretend you have to leave for something urgent, like we said, but instead of leaving the house you hide in the maid's room.

**CEO** – And then?

**Hostess** – After I get your Minister in an embarrassing situation, I call you, you come back without warning and you catch us in the act.

**CEO** – And then?

**Hostess** – Him! With your niece! You play the outraged uncle; you threaten to press charges. To call the press and give them all the details. He'll be willing to sign anything to make it go away ...

**CEO** – You're a genius!

*The minister returns. The hostess places the mop in a corner.*

**Hostess** – Please accept my apologies. I'm very sorry, I don't know what happened.

**Minister** – Don't mention it ...

**Hostess** – How about an after-dinner liqueur?

**CEO** – A little grope maybe? I mean, a little grappa?

**Hostess** – I promise not to drop it in your lap.

*The minister seems excited at this idea. The CEO pretends to take a call on his mobile phone.*

**CEO** – Yes? No? But that's awful ... Oh, my God! Yes, yes, of course, I'll be right there ... (*He puts his mobile phone away)* I am very sorry, Minister, but I am going to have to leave you for a while. My wife just had an accident ...

**Minister** – But that's dreadful. Is she alright?

**CEO** – Yes, well ... No ... The doctors don't know yet. They aren't sure if her wrist is broken or just sprained ...

**Minister** – In that case we'll have to continue this another time, of course.

**CEO** – No, really, please, I insist. I have a responsibility to my shareholders ... This contract is critical for the survival of the company ... I'll be back in a couple hours ...

**Minister** – Isn't she in Brighton?

**CEO** – Er ... No, actually she was already on her way back. Thankfully her accident happened near London ... She was already on the M25 ... My niece will keep you company until I get back ... Won't you Mirabelle…?

**Hostess** – Of course, Uncle ...

**Minister** – Well, in that case ... Very well ...

**Hostess** – Give Auntie all my love, Uncle ... I will pray for her speedy recovery ... (*The hostess walks the CEO to the door and talks to him quietly)* Promise to stay close by and come back as soon as I call you. Or I'm leaving right now.

**CEO** – I promise ... Here's my number ... (*To the minister)* Take care of my niece, Minister ...

*The CEO leaves.*

*The hostess, a little uncertain, turns to the minister.*

**Minister** – Alone, finally ...

**Hostess** – Yes ...

*The minister makes himself comfortable on the sofa.*

**Minister** – Why don't you come and sit with me and we'll talk about me ... I mean about you ... or maybe even about us?

*The hostess sits next to him reluctantly.*

**Minister** – I don't scare you, do I?

**Hostess** – No, not at all ... (*Hiding her discomfort)* I have to admit that ... I've been waiting for this moment all evening.

**Minister** – Really ...?

*The minister puts a hand on the hostess's shoulder.*

**Hostess** – I've always found powerful men very attractive ...

**Minister** – And yet, powerful men are still just men, you know ...

**Hostess** – Still ... To think that one day, if you are Prime Minister, you'll have the power to launch nuclear missiles ...

*The minister becomes even more eager.*

**Minister** – So that's what you want, huh? Nuclear missiles ...

*The hostess allows him to come a little closer but then extricates herself suddenly, grabs the contract from the table and holds it in the minister's face.*

**Hostess** – What if I asked you to sign this contract first?

**Minister** *(his mind elsewhere)* – The contract…?

**Hostess** – That way I can let Uncle know it's done and he can stay at my auntie's bedside all night if he wants to ...

**Minister** – For a sprained wrist?

**Hostess** – Given how late it is, they'll surely keep her under observation until tomorrow morning ... I'm sure that if I call my uncle now to tell him the contract is signed, we won't see him again tonight. We'll have the night to ourselves ...

**Minister** – Very well ... If it makes you happy, I'll sign this contract ... But there's no rush ...

*The minister gets up and picks up where he left off.*

**Hostess** – It won't take a second ... Please understand! The idea that my uncle could barge in at any second ... I can't get in the mood!

**Minister** – But I'd have to read it carefully, this contract ... I can't just sign anything willy nilly. Three billion pounds ...That's serious business, you know ...

**Hostess** – For me ... please ...

**Minister** – Please understand, Mirabelle! It takes time to read a hundred pages of dry legalese, and then having them initialled by the other party ... And that's not the kind of party I had in mind ...

**Hostess** – I think I hear someone coming up the stairs ...

**Minister** – I can't hear anything ...

*The minister tries again. The hostess evades him once again.*

**Hostess** – No really, I'm just too nervous ...

**Minister** – Come now, don't be a child ...

**Hostess** – I'm sorry but I can't. No signature, no ...

*The minister appears to relent.*

**Minister** – Fine, if that's what it takes to make you comfortable ... I won't even read it… After all, what's the worst that could happen ...? I trust your Uncle ... But you better brace yourself for my nuclear missile ...

*She hands him the document.*

**Hostess** – Here ...

*The minister is about to sign. His mobile phone rings. He puts the pen down.*

**Minister** – Can't a man get a moment's peace ... Please excuse me. I have to take this or my Private Secretary will send a Special Ops team ... And if you think your uncle interrupting us is bad ...

**Hostess** – But of course ...

*He takes the call and the hostess can rest a moment.*

**Minister** – Yes ... No? When? No, no, I'm listening ...

*After motioning to the hostess to excuse him, he goes into the room next door looking for privacy. She grabs her mobile phone.*

**Hostess** – Are you in the room? Great. No, I was just checking. No, not yet. I'll call you when we're ready. But keep your mobile with you, okay? (*The minister returns and the hostess hastily puts her mobile away)* Everything okay?

**Minister** – Nothing important ... Nothing that would get in the way of what we were doing anyway.

*The minister tries to pick up where he left off.*

**Hostess** – You haven't signed the contract yet ...

**Minister** (*his mind elsewhere)* – What contract…? Oh, yes, the contract ... But don't worry about that ... It's not relevant anymore ...

**Hostess** – Not relevant anymore?

**Minister** – I just got a call from my Private Secretary ... What I'm about to tell you is classified, Mirabelle ... Can I count on your discretion?

**Hostess** – How can you even doubt me?

**Minister** – The Education Minister just got arrested by the police in a compromising situation with an under-aged prostitute in the red-light district. In all probability, he'll have to resign ...

**Hostess** – What has the world come to ... If we can't even entrust our children's future to sexual predators anymore ... But how does that affect our little business with the contract? Don't tell me you were planning on extending the Ealing-Ashbocking motorway with a slip road going through the red-light district?

**Minister** – It's the butterfly effect, my dear child! The blowjob that broke the camel's back ...

**Hostess** – How do you mean ...?

**Minister** – A resignation means a cabinet reshuffle. Which is basically a game of musical chairs. The waltz of the portfolios. And unfortunately ... there won't be a chair for me this time around.

**Hostess** – Oh shit ... I mean, blast ...

**Minister** – Anyway, I think it's probably best if I took a step back before the next General Elections ... I'll have more free time for myself ... and for you!

**Hostess** – Ah yes, but this is all quite unfortunate ...

**Minister** – I love this old-fashioned way you have of speaking, Mirabelle ... Did you really study in a girls-only boarding school? Why don't you tell me more about that ...

**Hostess** – And what about the contract ...?

**Minister** – Naturally, it's out of the question that I sign anything now. My successor will handle it. But I'm not sure he'll be as interested as I am in a direct route between Ealing and Ashbocking… When I'm Prime Minister ... maybe ...

**Hostess** – If you ever get there ...

**Minister** – Either way, now we have the whole evening to ourselves, no more interruptions ...

*The hostess can't find any more reasons to reject the minister.*

**Hostess** – Very well ... So here's what I suggest ... Go take a shower, make yourself comfortable ... And I'll do the same ... But first I'll call my uncle to tell him he shouldn't worry about this contract anymore ... Okay?

**Minister** – Okay ... Can you point me in the direction of the bathroom?

**Hostess** – Er ...

**Minister** – Never mind, I went there earlier when you spilled Champagne all over my lap ...

**Hostess** – So you know where it is as well as I do ...

**Minister** – Won't be a minute ... I'll be right back ...

*The minister leaves. The hostess quickly grabs her mobile phone.*

**Hostess** – Are you kidding me… Out of battery ... (*She rummages in her bag)* And of course I don't have my charger ... (*She thinks for a bit)* I don't have time to find the maid's room either. I'll get lost in this huge mansion ... Wait, he said it was right above us ...

*The hostess takes the mop. She stands on the table and hits the ceiling in a rhythm of quick and long pauses, like morse code (this can be a sound effect played in the theater)*

**Minister** (*off)* – Yes, yes, coming ... No need to be in such a hurry ...

**Hostess** – Oh shit ...

*The minister returns wearing only a ridiculous dressing gown. He sees the hostess standing on the table. He takes the opportunity to sneak a peek under her skirt.*

**Minister** – I love women who aren't afraid of a little DIY ... Do you need a hand?

**Hostess** – I'm just changing a lightbulb ... There, it's done ... I ... I tried calling my uncle but ... I'm out of battery.

**Minister** – My batteries are 100% charged, believe me!

**Hostess** – Excellent ... Could I maybe borrow your mobile so I can call him ...

*To get to her, the minister starts climbing on the table.*

**Minister** – Never mind your uncle ... He won't be back any time soon ... He only just left ...

**Hostess** – It's just that ... I haven't told you everything, John ...

*That calms the minister down a bit.*

**Minister** – Oh really ...?

**Hostess** – I'm not really Adam Sugar's niece ...

*The minister takes it in but doesn't appear that surprised.*

**Minister** – Actually, I suspected as such ...

**Hostess** – Oh really ...?

**Minister** – I've been around the block a few times, you know ...

**Hostess** – Of course ...

**Minister** – You're his lover, of course.

**Hostess** – His lover ... Yes, that's it ...

**Minister** – Don't worry about it! I'm not jealous!

*He's about to start again, but she stops him.*

**Hostess** – Yes, but he is ...

**Minister** – But he'll never know.

**Hostess** – No, but I will!

**Minister** – So?

**Hostess** – I must break up with him first, before ... starting a relationship with you, do you understand?

**Minister** – Yes ... Actually, no!

**Hostess** – Let me call him, please! I'll feel a lot better and I can give myself more entirely to you.

**Minister** – More entirely ...

**Hostess** – Will you let me borrow your phone?

**Minister** – All right ...

*He hands her his phone. She takes it, still on the table. But the minister isn't showing any signs of giving her privacy for the call.*

**Hostess** – I'll send him a text message. I don't have the heart to tell him directly. Especially now with his wife in hospital ...

**Minister** – Of course ...

*She pretends to read the text message she's typing.*

**Hostess** – I'm leaving you ... (*Quietly*) Come quick ... There, that's done ...

*She climbs down from the table. The minister grabs her immediately. She quickly climbs back on the table and keeps him in check with the mop.*

**Hostess** – No, I'm going to wait for his reply, to be sure he received the message ... before giving myself to you ...

**Minister** – Oh no you don't, I can't wait any longer ...

*The minister grabs the hostess's legs, who is still standing on the table. The CEO bursts into the room, faking surprise and reacting with feigned outrage.*

**CEO** – Minister! You? In a dressing gown! With my niece! In my own house! And to think I had absolute trust in you!

*The minister, also taken by surprise, stops the assault immediately. But he soon comes to his senses.*

**Minister** – All right ... You can stop this charade… I know everything… Mirabelle told me ...

**CEO** – You know everything?

**Minister** – Everything. But I'm not sure this poor child understands the details of your odious plan.

**CEO** – This poor child?

**Minister** – I also imagine you weren't in hospital with your wife ...

**CEO** – Er ... No ... I was just upstairs, with the maid ...

**Minister** – You disappoint me greatly, my friend ... It's none of my business if you're sleeping with the maid ... But using this innocent and vulnerable young woman to further your dark ambitions ...

**CEO** – So you haven't signed the contract ...

**Minister** – That's what it was all about, wasn't it? You arranged for me to be left alone with your mistress, knowing full well she wouldn't be able to resist my charms.

**CEO** – My mistress?

**Minister** – And to be forgiven, I would have signed the contract.

**CEO** *(regaining some hope)* – And that's what you're going to do, isn't it? Because we all know you're nothing if not a gentleman ...

**Minister** – That's very petty of you ... But I might have done it, it's true ... Because, as you point out, I am a gentleman. Unfortunately, I am not in a position to do so any longer ...

**CEO** – In position ...?

**Minister** – I am not Transport Minister any longer. I'll mention your contract to my successor. But I can't guarantee anything.

**CEO** – You're not a minister anymore?

**Minister** – This really isn't your day, my friend ... Not only will your contract not get signed, but your mistress has decided to leave you for me. Come, Mirabelle, let's go ...

*The CEO explodes.*

**CEO** – Mirabelle? You dirty old bastard! This girl isn't my niece, that's true. But she isn't my lover either. She's a hooker!

**Minister** – A hooker?

**Hostess** – A hooker?

**CEO** – Did you think your natural charm would be enough to seduce a girl thirty years younger?

**Minister** – Why not?

**CEO** – And you really think that if this girl was my lover she'd prefer you over me?

**Minister** – Miss, say something ...

**Hostess** – I'm not a hooker!

**CEO** – That's right, I'm sorry ...

**Minister** – What are you talking about?

**CEO** – Let's say she's more like ... an escort. You know what it's like nowadays, the unemployed are job seekers, secretaries are assistants and hookers are escorts!

**Hostess** – I'm not an escort either!

**CEO** – Oh that's right, you prefer sex worker ...

**Hostess** – I'll remind you that I ended up here due to a misunderstanding ...

**Minister** – It would appear I did too ... And this is all turning out to be rather complicated. So, who are you, exactly?

**Hostess** – Your worst nightmare!

**Minister** – Am I to understand that you won't be leaving with me?

**Hostess** – In your dreams ... And with what I have on you now, you horny bastard, I can easily ruin your political career.

**Minister** – Come now, Mirabelle ...

**Hostess** – Stop calling me Mirabelle! My name is Emmanuelle.

**Minister** – Oh, really ... You don't look like an Emmanuelle…

**CEO** – That's exactly what I said ...

**Hostess** – Shut up!

**Minister** – That'll tell him ...

**Hostess** – You too! You're just a moronic sex pest! You were ready to sign a contract without reading it because there was a chance it might lead to sleeping with a woman who could be your daughter, and you were hoping to become the next Prime Minister?

**Minister** – You're using the past tense, am I to understand this means you're planning on preventing the achievement of my personal career goals?

**Hostess** – I learned a lot about politics tonight. Probably more than I ever will during my entire studies at the London School of Economics. So yes, I'll have a lot to say to whoever will ask me. And I consider it a service to our nation to make sure you crawl back under your rock in Suffolk ...

**CEO** – There, there, calm down, please ... I think we've all gotten a bit carried away… I'm sure we can find some mutual ground. Can't we, Minister?

**Hostess** – I am not a whore but you're a pimp, and you're a dirty old pig! That's what I think of your contract (*She tears up the contract)* And if you think I'm going to give you back the money you paid me you've got another thing coming. I earned it!

**Minister** – So you did pay her?

**CEO** – It's a little complicated ...

**Minister** – Don't tell me she's actually your niece ... (*The minister's mobile phone rings and he takes the call)* Yes…? No? Okay. All right ... No, no, I'll call you back in a minute ... Yes, yes, everything's fine ...

*He puts his mobile phone away.*

**Hostess** – You think everything's fine?

**Minister** – Turns out I'm keeping my minister position. The Crown Prosecutor is a friend of the Prime Minister. He's going to see to it that the situation doesn't become public knowledge ...

**CEO** – So you're back in a position to sign this contract ...

**Minister** – Yes, I am ...

**Hostess** – Too late! I just tore it up ...

**Minister** – I imagine you can print out another copy ...

**CEO** – Of course.

**Minister** – This might come as a surprise, given everything that went on tonight, but I'm going to sign this contract, and then I'll leave you to sort out your family affairs in private ...

**Hostess** – But why?

**Minister** – Because it's a fair contract, that's why. And I came here with the intention of signing it anyway.

**Hostess** – But what about the competitor?

**Minister** – There is no competitor. At least none that are seriously in competition with your proposal. I was also trying to screw you.

**CEO** – Congratulations, Minister. A negotiation is just a poker game where all parties try to bluff each other. However, I think it's now time to put an end to all of this. Believe me, this is win-win situation.

**Hostess** – And what do I win?

*The CEO provides another copy of the contract and while the minister signs it, the CEO pulls out a cigar box, takes one out and offers one to the minister.*

**CEO** – Cigar?

**Minister** – There isn't a cliché you won't embrace, is there?

*The CEO takes the cigar from his mouth, puts it back in the box then puts the box away.*

**CEO** – I imagine you don't have an ageing mother in an assisted living facility in Framlingham either.

**Minister** – Not a mother, no ... But a young woman close to my heart ...

**CEO** – I see ... And an extension to the motorway would have brought her closer to your ... Let's talk again after the General Elections ...

**Minister** (*with a worried look towards the hostess)* – I'm not even sure I'll be in the running ...

**CEO** – It will be fine! You know what they say, the road to success is paved with good extensions!

*The minister is about to leave.*

**CEO** – About my MBE ...? (*The minister glares at him).* You're right, I don't think I've earned it yet ... I think I'll wait until I am truly worthy of this honor ...

**Minister** – As our young friend here would say ... Don't underestimate yourself, my friend ... If you knew the number of dictators, drug traffickers and crooks who make it onto the Honors List ...

**CEO** – That's true ... When it comes to honor, the UK lost its AAA rating a long time ago.

**Minister** – Can I drop you somewhere…?

**Hostess** – Thank you, but no, I've just about seen enough of you ...

**Minister** – Are you sure you want to destroy my political career? Better the devil you know. How do you know the rest aren't worse?

**Hostess** – I'm trying to imagine ... I'm struggling ...

**Minister** – Please ... I beg for your forgiveness, there.

**Hostess** – How much is my silence worth to you?

**Minister** – What did you have in mind?

*The hostess thinks for a bit then whispers something in his ear.*

**Minister** – Very well, consider it done ...

**CEO** – Can I call you a cab?

**Minister** – I think I'll walk.

*He leaves. The CEO remains alone with the hostess.*

**Hostess** – I'll be on my way too ...

**CEO** – I beg your forgiveness, too. Times are hard, you know. We're in an economical crisis ...

**Hostess** – Even the CEOs are affected ...

**CEO** – Please let me pay you the rest of the fee. I insist. After all, the contract is signed, which was the objective. You fulfilled your mission ...

**Hostess** – But he was going to sign it anyway ...

**CEO** – That's true, but well ... I owe you for what I put you through ...

**Hostess** – Keep the other half of the money ... What the Minister just promised me is enough, we'll call it even ...

*The doorbell rings.*

**CEO** – What does this moron want now ...?

*He goes to the flat's intercom.*

**CEO** – Yes ...? Yes, yes ... No, of course ... Not at all, I'll let you in right now ...

*He returns.*

**CEO** – Oh God, it's my wife!

**Hostess** – She's not in Brighton?

**CEO** – Apparently after the mixup on the phone earlier, she decided to come home early ... What an evening! And then there's the business with the maid ...

**Hostess** – What business with the maid ...?

**CEO** – She came back earlier than planned too ... When she found me in her room she thought I was waiting for her and she almost raped me ...

**Hostess** – Poetic justice is beautiful: you now have first hand experience of what you put me through tonight ...

**CEO** – How do I explain to my wife that I'm at home with a prostitute ...

**Hostess** – For the last time, I am not a prostitute!

**CEO** – You think it's easier to explain the presence of a student ...? I told you before, she's very jealous. You have to help me out of this mess. Just tell her you're ... I don't know ... My niece!

**Hostess** – That's your plan?

**CEO** – Never mind, we'll improvise. You seem to have quite the talent for it ... Right, I'm going downstairs to let her in ...

*The hostess immediately grabs her mobile phone.*

**Hostess** – Isabelle? No, I'm still with your client, I'll tell you everything later ... What about you, where are you? Ivan? The CEO of Woodwall? Oh, I see, it was all a set-up ... You thought that if you sent me here I wouldn't be able to seduce the Minister, creating an opportunity for you to finish the job when he came over later ... Yeah, well, good luck with that ... Well, because he just signed the contract, that's why! What was that about my power of seduction again? And you know what else? He's going to put me on the next Honor's List for an MBE! Listen, I'd love to stay and chat but I've got to go, the evening isn't quite over yet. I think the nation still needs my help ...

**CEO** – Honey, listen, please calm down! You can ask her yourself. You'll see, it's all very simple ...

*Fade to black as God Save The Queen plays.*

***The End***

*August 2022*

www.ingramcontent.com/pod-product-compliance
Lightning Source LLC
LaVergne TN
LVHW010507160826
845677LV00012B/2711

*9782377058082*